HO'
THE

The First Deed ... Cuchulain
who was the greatest warrior that ever lived

Adapted and illustrated by P S Hoben

Best Wishes
P S Hobe

First published in 2013

P S Hoben

1

ISBN-13 978-1490382951

for Jack

PROLOGUE

When Setanta was a baby, just two years of age, he was caught up in the middle of a peculiar incident. He was out in the woods with his father Sualtaim, who was hunting for wild grouse. Sualtaim was keeping a good eye on the child, because they were passing close to a treacherous gorge.

Sualtaim had taken up a hiding-place behind an outgrowth of ferns, and was crouched, with his slingshot in his hand, loaded and ready to fire. There they hid, man and boy, neither of them making a sound, waiting for a bird to emerge.

Suddenly, a wild deer burst out of the undergrowth behind them, and bounded right over their heads. Sualtaim grabbed Setanta and pulled him close. The deer leapt right across the gorge. It disappeared under the trees on the far side of the water. In the same moment, the first of a huge pack of hunting dogs came through, chasing after the deer. More and more dogs appeared so that within no time, the clearing was awash with sweat and fur.

Then the hunters arrived. The men shouted and whistled to their animals, trying to bring them under control. The dogs swirled in circles all around them, sniffing the ground, crashing through branches, yelping and growling and barking and yapping.

In the middle of all this commotion, Sualtaim took his eye off the child for just a second. When he looked back to where Setanta had been standing just a moment before, the baby was gone! Sualtaim's heart jumped up through his chest and stopped in his throat. Frantic with panic, he ran in circles around the place, waving his arms, screaming, "Setanta! Setanta! Setanta!"

But Setanta had wandered off towards the edge of the ravine, and had squeezed himself through a gap between two rocks. The opening led down towards the water. After slipping through, Setanta slid on his backside all the way down the steep bank, sending little avalanches of dirt in front of him, until he landed in a heap at the bottom, smeared in mud from head to toe, balanced right at the edge of the swirling, roaring waters.

Meanwhile at the top of the ravine,

Sualtaim and the hunters were desperately searching for the child, shouting his name. All but one of the hunting-dogs were by now at heel. But the one that remained on the loose was their leader. He was the oldest, the strongest, the most cruel of all of the pack dogs; a vicious, merciless killer, who would make an easy snack of the boy without even stopping first to lick his chops. Right at that moment, his black eyes were locked on the muddy little baby, who was sitting helpless at the water's edge, hidden from the search-party high above him, and totally oblivious to his peril.

At the top of the gorge, still looking for the missing toddler, Sualtaim and the men heard the sound of howling and screeching coming from below. They knew immediately what it meant. All the men dived towards the sound, desperate to reach the stricken child.

Sualtaim was the first to arrive, but the scene that met him was not the one he was expecting:

The baby was standing at the bank of the river, smiling up at them innocently. Behind the child, floating in the water, was the limp shape of a drowned dog. The current was rushing over the body, trying to wash it downstream, but the dead beast was snagged against a rock.

Sualtaim, his panic now washed away in a flood of relief, grabbed the tiny boy up into his arms and squeezed him tight against his chest until the child squealed to be let free.

But the lead hunter looked shocked, "I have never heard of a dog killed like that! They don't just slip and drown— ever. Something did this. To overpower that old hound, it must have had some strength, whatever it was. It must have come out of those woods, attacked the dog, and disappeared again."

Sualtaim answered, "There are monsters that live in the woods of Oircil— this is known. I have even heard that the lair of the Morrigna is hidden somewhere in there. Whether that is true or not, I don't care a bit. My boy is alive, that is all I care about— however it happened."

So, Sualtaim and Setanta returned to their home and to the boy's mother Deichtire without *a grouse to cook. The huntsmen returned to their homes without any deer. Instead, that night, they each brought back a fine story to tell.*

Yet the mystery of how the baby was saved from death that day was never truly explained. Perhaps Setanta himself witnessed what happened at the foot of the gorge. But he was too young to speak of it, or even to understand it. Later, when the boy was older, his father would sometimes ask him about it, but Setanta was never able to remember a thing.

PREFACE

This is the story of the boyhood deeds of Cuchulain, who was truly the greatest warrior that the world has ever seen. He was fiercer than the mighty Achilles, who tore down the walls of the city of Troy; stronger than Hercules, who captured the wild Bull of Crete; braver even than Leonidas, King of Sparta, who made his last stand before the gates of Greece, and there defied the hordes of Persia, whose numbers were vast beyond counting.

It is an old story, one that has been told often by bards and by scholars. This telling is a simple one, for a young man who lives just a spear's throw from where Cuchulain achieved his most infamous deeds. Not in ancient Greece or Rome, but in Ireland: at the Gap of the North, beside the Ring of Gullion, in County Armagh.

Now if this tale sometimes grows too tall to believe— remember that it took place a very, very long time ago. It was a time when the valleys of Ireland were dark with forests. Under the cover of those ancient trees, wild deer hid and wolves hunted. But in the darkest places lurked stranger things still.

This was a time long before the Saint arrived to banish all of the monsters and magical things; before he slammed shut the doors leading into the underground world of the Sidhe and locked them forever.

But I promise you this: every word of it is true and no word of it is a lie.

HOUND OF THE ULAID

THE WARRIOR SCHOOL

etanta was just five years old when he heard some boys talking about the magnificent fort of King Conchobar at Emain Macha, the great city of the Ulaid (which is today called Navan Fort in County Armagh.)

Now, Conchobar mac Nessa was King of the Ulaid. This was the name used by the people of the kingdom of Uladh, which was the northernmost of the five kingdoms of Erin.

The boys said they were going to join the warrior school at Emain Macha, where they would be taught how to fight with swords and how to throw spears. They would learn how to be fearless in battle. At the end of their training, they would take up arms to join the king's army and fight alongside his champions.

On hearing this, Setanta went to his mother and said, "I will go to join the warrior school."

Deichtire smiled, "You will surely go there little man, when you are old enough. King Conchobar, your uncle, will send a champion to bring you there safely. It is a long journey and a dangerous one too."

"I won't wait for that! I'll go there myself sooner. Which way is it?"

"It is too far a distance for that, impatient little man. It is a long way north, far past Sliabh Fuait. Now forget about it and get to bed."

But the boy didn't forget about it. The next morning he woke up before the sun came up and he set out alone.

With him he took his toy wooden shield, his hurley stick and his little bronze ball. He took his short javelin spears for throwing and his toy-staff with its fire-hardened butt-end. With these he made up a game to shorten the length of his journey.

He would give the ball a whack with the hurl-bat, so that he sent it flying a long way ahead of him. Then with a second throw he would launch the hurley out after it. He would fire his darts, let fly his toy–staff, then make a wild chase after all of them. Next he would scoop up his hurl–bat and catch the ball on the end of it and snatch up the darts. But the stock of the toy–staff had not touched the ground when he caught its tip which was still in the air.

By this way he made it to Emain Macha.

SOME WELCOME HE GOT

etanta arrived at Emain Macha as the sun was setting. The towers of the great stone fort cast long shadows across the playing fields where the boy–troop were.

Three times fifty of them there were: boys no younger than ten years, with most of them a good bit older than that. Some of them were running through their drills; throwing war spears at sack–men stuffed with straw, or stabbing at them with short blades.

Most of the boy-troop were playing together in a great game of hurling. When Setanta saw this he burst onto the pitch into the midst of the boys. He whipped the ball between his two legs away from them. He didn't let the ball get above his knee, nor did he let it drop below his ankle. He drove it forward, holding it between his two legs, so that not one of the boys was able to get a prod or a stroke or a blow or a shot at it. He carried it over the goal whooping and laughing past them all. The boys all gazed upon him, amazed.

Now, the leader of the troop, Follaman, who was King Conchobar's son, was proud, and his pride was sorely hurt at this intrusion.

"Come on lads," he shouted, "this dirty wee brat has insulted us with his tricks! He came in here uninvited and just wrecked the game. Now throw yourselves all on him. Batter the life out of him! Don't listen to his begging. Kill him stone dead!"

So all three times fifty of them set upon him. They threw their hurleys at him, but he weaved and dived and pushed them all away, so that not one of them harmed him.

Then they fired their three times fifty balls at his head, but he raised his arms and the palms of his hands against them. He caught all the balls, balancing them on his chest. Then he launched them back, twice as hard, so that each ball hit the same boy that had thrown it. Half of the boys were knocked to the ground while the other half started to cry like babies with the pain.

"Kill him!" roared Follaman. He picked up his long war spear and launched it with full force at the lad's heart. But Setanta caught the dart on his wooden shield. Then all three times fifty boys fired their spears. But he jumped up, span clear of the first lot, and caught the rest on his shield where they stuck. He yanked each one out, snapped it in half then stamped on the halves, smashing them all into splinters.

Suddenly, the *Battle Rage* came over him:

His body shook and became twisted and contorted. His face grew red and purple and blew up like a balloon. His hair all stuck out straight on end. It was as if each hair was hammered into his head. At the tip of each hair a spark lit up. One of his eyes popped open bigger than the mouth of a cup; the other he squeezed as tight as the eye of a needle. He opened his mouth wide to his jawbone so that his gullet could be seen shaking with anger. He let a big roar out of him like twenty lions. Out of the crown of his head the warrior's light rose up: white and neon and violet.

His fury was terrible to see. The nearest fifty of the boys fainted at the sight of him. The furthest fifty of them ran wailing for their lives; while the last fifty stood stuck to the spot, their legs wobbling underneath them, refusing to budge. Follaman wet himself.

Setanta burst forward, scattering the boys to the ground where they were standing, then went screaming after the rest.

Now King Conchobar was at the training ground that day. He was in his tent playing a game of chess with Fergus mac Roth, who was the king's foster father, and who once was king himself.

"What in the name of Brigit is that racket outside?" asked Conchobar, just as five of the boys burst into the tent, and dashed headlong past the men where they sat. Hard on their tails was Setanta. He leapt into the air and landed on top of the chessboard, knocking the pieces flying everywhere. Conchobar grabbed him by the wrist.

"What is going on here, fierce little man? This is some rough game you are playing!"

"It should be!" answered Setanta, "I arrived here tonight as a stranger but it is not a stranger's welcome I got. A thief's welcome more like!"

"What do you call yourself?" asked the king.

"I am Setanta, son of Deichtire and Sualtaim. I came to join the warrior school."

"Did you indeed? You are the spit of your mother!" said the king, now laughing, "Did you not know that it is forbidden for a stranger to join the boy–troop in their games, without first asking their protection?"

"I did not."

"I see. Follaman, son, take your cousin Setanta now under your protection and the protection of the troop."

"Surely I will, father. No harm will come to

him from us or from any other while he is here." Follaman bowed to his father. The boys took Setanta with them as they left.

The boy troop began their game again. This time Setanta played with their permission and under their protection.

But no sooner had the game begun when he rushed at the boys again. He boxed them, with front blows and mid blows and long blows. He knocked them down then threw them sideways. He twisted their arms behind their backs.

Fifty of them he floored in this way before the king roared, "Stop! What are you doing now?"

Setanta answered, "I swear they all now must ask to come under *my* protection, just as I had to come under theirs. Otherwise I shall not lay off them until I have knocked down every last one of them."

"Well, wee hard man. By my command, your uncle and your king, do that now. Give them your protection."

"I will."

So the boy–troop went under Setanta's protection from that moment on.

THE STONE BED

etanta was given a bed at Emain Macha. Being the nephew of the king, he had a room for himself. But he wasn't able to sleep. Instead, he would lie awake in his bed all night.

"Tell me," Conchobar said to him, "why is it you can't sleep at night?"

"I can't sleep unless my bed is level, with it the same height at my head as it is at my feet."

So Conchobar had a pillar stone set up at the boy's head with another at his feet. His bed was hung between them so that he could lie level. He slept well at night after that.

Now one time, Setanta slept in late. So a man was sent into his room to wake him. But before he had woken up and knew what he was doing, the boy lashed out. He punched the man so hard that his fist went right through the man's head and came out the other side with the man's brain stuck on it. Then the fist went onwards into the stone pillar and split it in half.

After that day, no-one dared to go in to wake the boy, so he got up whenever he wanted.

A LINE WAS DRAWN

nother time, the boys were playing a game of hurling. Setanta was alone on one side. There were three times fifty boys playing against him on the other side. But the sun was low. It shone into his eyes. It kept blinding him so that he lost the game.

But losing the game brought the Battle Rage on him. He laid into the boys with his fists. He beat fifty of them so badly that he left them with broken bones.

One of them got a punch in the head so hard that he was dead before he hit the ground. Seeing what he had caused, Setanta escaped. Afterwards he hid in fear of what his punishment would be.

He ran into the hall where the king's champions were sitting around. He squeezed himself under the couch where no-one could reach him. When the champions heard what he had done they demanded that he come out to face the king's justice, but he stayed put. So they started to pull the couch up off the ground to get at him; but the boy grabbed it from beneath and held it down, until there were thirty men around the couch, all pulling and shoving and shaking at it with all their strength. Still Setanta, with just his own strength, held it down.

Then he stood up, lifting the couch above his head with the thirty champions piled on top of it. He bore it out of the hall into the middle of the fort.

There the champions jumped down. They surrounded the boy. They captured him and held him fast until his wrath came down. He was brought before the king who made his pronouncement.

"What have you done?" asked King Conchobar.

"I lost the game, so I lost the head. But those lads paid the price for that."

"It is a grave act you have confessed to,

young man. You have broken your promise of protection on your fellows. You have put terrible suffering on the loved ones of the boy who you killed in your madness.

That boy was loved by his mother just as you are by yours!

"The law of Uladh demands this: For the crime of killing another by violence, the punishment is death!"

Turning to address his court, Conchobar continued, "But it is beyond the authority of even the king to destroy the gods' gift to the Ulaid: sent by the Sidhe to be the deadliest foe of our foes; to be our sole protector at the hour of our greatest peril! By the same decree, fate will not suffer this child of unnatural powers to be chained or caged.

"Yet it is my duty to protect all those under my care. In this I have failed. More than this, it is no good at all for the country, that half of our future champions might be crippled before they even take up arms!

"My judgement is this:

"Setanta, you will leave Emain Macha. You will return to your home where you will stay for one year. During this time you will look into your heart to discover whether you are able keep your bond of protection. When you return, you will make a solemn, binding oath before your king and your fellows: to use your gifts always and only for the good of the kingdom of Uladh. You will do this or suffer banishment from the boy–troop and from the country forever."

In this way, Setanta was removed from the warrior school and returned home in shame.

THE OAK HOUSE

etanta spent his sixth year at home, with his mother Deichtire and his father Sualtaim at the Oak House, which was at the northern edge of the plain of Muirthemne (which is today called Dundalk.)

He stayed there through Summer and Autumn and Winter and Spring. At the end of this time, on the last night of Spring, Setanta had a curious dream. He woke up and climbed into his parents' bed.

"What is it wee man?" asked Deichtire.

"I had a dream. I was at Emain Macha. The king was there but he was younger than he is now. There were flags flying. Then hundreds of birds with long necks flew over. I flew up to them. We went over the land, far away. Then there was a doorway and a room. There were tall, strange people. There was light glowing all around them. Then there was a woman. She was holding a baby and she lifted it up to her cheek and showed it to me. She was smiling."

Deichtire put her arm around him and said,

"Setanta, my love. That was no ordinary dream! It was a vision of the past you saw! This is how it happened:

Ten years ago, in the middle of the night, the young women who were living at Emain Macha all disappeared. The king sent his men the length and breadth of the country to look for them but they were nowhere to be found. Three years the men spent searching, calling out their names; but they caught neither sight nor sound of the girls. In the end, the people of Emain Macha had started to give up hope of ever seeing their missing daughters alive.

Then one summer evening, a great flock of geese flew in from the south. The birds landed. They started eating up all the wheat that was growing in the fields until there were nothing but empty stalks left. The king commanded his guard to hunt down the birds before they destroyed the whole crop. But the men couldn't catch or kill any of them. Every time one of the men got close enough to fire a shot, the birds flew off and landed again further away, just out of reach.

The men raced after the birds, following them deep into the haunted land beyond Brú na Bóinne, where the hidden houses of the Sidhe are, who people call the Ever-Young. But a fog rose up from the river. The birds disappeared into the thick of it. So, being far from Emain Macha, and hardly able to see each other through the fog, the men made camp for the night.

One of the men was Brichtu, Poison-Tongue. He went out alone into the mist but soon got lost. He wandered around blindly, calling out; listening for *the shouts of his companions, but heard nothing.*

Then he caught a glimmer of the music of harps, coming and going; echoing all around so that his heart fainted with the beauty of it. The melody led him gently, drawing him deeper into the grey until found himself standing at the door of a magnificent house built of wood and stone. Decorating the doorway was a carved pattern of many birds flying in formation. A warm light shone out. There was the sound of footsteps and laughter coming from within.

He stepped inside. There, to his amazement, he looked upon the missing daughters of Emain Macha. Some were huddled together talking; others were moving around lightly, dancing with the strange people of the Sidhe: the Tuath Dé Danann.

One of the women was holding a

newborn baby. She stepped forward and raised her hand in welcome.

The woman spoke: 'Come Brichtu, rest with us. At last you have found what was missing. Tomorrow we will all return home to Emain together.

'With us we have a wonderful gift to bring, for the good of all of the Ulaid:'

She turned the child to show Brichtu his little pink face. It was only then that Brichtu recognized the woman as Deichtire, the sister of the king...

Then Deichtire laughed, "So you see, little man, the woman you saw in your dream was me, your mother. The child you saw was yourself. That was how you came into the world, my love."

THE CURSE OF MACHA

etanta settled back to sleep but before long he was awake again. He ran back into Deichtire and woke her,

"Mother, I had another dream. This one was worse."

"Climb into the bed beside me and tell me about it," she said.

"I dreamt that the king and the champions and all the Ulaid were marching to war. They had banners. They carried their spears and their tall shields. Then they all fell to the ground and starting rolling around. They had their knees curled up to their chests. They were wailing and screaming. Not one of them could stand up.

"But the enemy army came running in. There were a hundred times fifty of them. They charged over the plain towards us, and there was only me left standing to face them."

"Setanta, my little hero! What you dreamt was a vision of the future. In your vision, the Ulaid are suffering under the curse of Macha. Only you are immune to it because of how you came into the world. Let me tell you how the men of the Ulaid came under the curse:

There once was a rich farmer called Cruinn. He had four sons around him. But his wife, the mother of his children, died. For a long time after this he lived alone with her memory, and brought up his sons without a woman about the place.

One day, a tall woman walked into his house, dressed in the fine clothes of a queen. She sat herself down on a chair near the fire. She passed the whole day there without saying a word with anyone. When evening came, she went to the kitchen and prepared a meal for Cruinn and his sons. She watched them eat, without speaking. Later, she put the young sons into their beds and returned back to the hearth to put out the fire. Finally she spoke:

'Cruinn, since your wife passed away, you have honoured her memory. But she has made a wish that I come to you with this message: your sons are lacking the love of a mother, and you yourself are in need a wife. These things I could be. Will you refuse me?'

'I will not,' he replied.

'Then I will gladly stay with you. But be warned— no living person can know that I am here, or our time together will be at an end.'

'I will say no word about you to anyone,' he promised.

So she became his wife and for a long time they dwelt together peacefully and in love.

..

Sometime later, the King of Uladh

announced he would hold a festival. He called all his subjects to attend.

'Do not go, Cruinn!' begged his wife. 'You will surely let slip some word of my being here!'

'I must go my love. But don't worry! I will not make a whisper of you to anyone.'

At the festival, the king made a parade of his finest horses. He raced them against each other. The fastest of them were Gaoithbán the White Wind, and Sciobtha the Swift.

'Never before have two horses such as these been seen in all of Erin!' declared the racemaster.

Cruinn nudged the arm of the man standing next to him, 'Sure my wife can run faster than either of those two horses,' he joked.

But to Cruinn's alarm, the man

repeated the joke, and from there it spread until it reached the ears of the king himself.

Furious, the king announced, 'Such mockery! Seize the man that dared to say this. Hold him until his wife can be brought here to race!'

Messengers were sent to the home of Cruinn. They summoned his wife to the festival.

'Your husband has boasted that you run faster than the swiftest of the king's horses. You must come with us now to prove this claim.'

'My husband is a twit to say such a thing. I cannot race in my condition. Look at me! I am about to give birth to a child!'

But the messengers warned her, 'That is a shame; for if you will not come then your husband will be killed.'

"Then I will go with you and I will speak to the king myself."

She arrived at the parade where the crowds received her with jeers.

She addressed the king, 'Mighty King! It is not right that I should be stared at and laughed at by your people in the state I am in! Why have you brought me here?'

The king sneered, 'To mock a woman is to dishonour her. But your honour is beneath my concern.

'To mock a king— is to rake the hackles of the lion! Now you must choose: race against the best of my horses; or your husband will pay for his folly.'

'Please, you cannot ask me to race today. Will you not wait until my child arrives? I promise you, after that I will give you your race.'

But the king was unmoved, 'Guards, bring your swords and kill this woman's fool of a husband.'

'Help me someone!' she cried to the bystanders. 'Please have mercy on me. A mother gave birth to each one of you!'

But not one of them would aid her. 'Race! Race! Race!' they shouted.

'Shame on you all. You show no pity or respect for me. I am Macha of the Tuath Dé Danann! From this day and forever, my name will be over this place. Now bring the horses and I will do what you ask.'

So the horses were brought and she ran against them. She outran them easily and won the race by a long way.

But at the finish line she cried out a dreadful scream. She fell to the ground in agony. All of the men who heard her cries were suddenly seized with weakness, so that they had no more strength than the woman herself in her pangs of childbirth.

Her husband rushed to her side and right there she bore him twins. But after her labour her strength was all spent.

Then she cursed them:

Cruel men of Uladh!
Little mercy have you shown.
The seeds of your misfortune
Your misogyny has sown!

Spiteful men of Uladh!
Your mothers you forgot;
When three times I begged for pity
But heed me you did not!

Wicked men of Uladh,
Sorry you will be!
Nine generations will you rue
The day you harried me!

For five long days and nights between
Your bodies will be sore.
You'll know full well, by sharp reprise,
The pain your mothers bore!

Thus, as the twins of Macha are,
You too shall be indeed:
Robbed of all protection
At your hour of greatest need!

44

Then Macha spoke no more. She closed her eyes. Cruinn cradled her in his arms. She died.

With this, Deichtire finished her story:

"So you see, little man: on that day, the city of the Ulaid took the name *Emain Macha*, which means 'the Twins of Macha'. Meanwhile the men of the Ulaid remain cursed by the Pangs to this very day.

"Because of this, Setanta, the time will come when you alone must defend the kingdom from her enemies. You must hold fast for five days and four nights, until the curse runs its course, until the Pangs of the Ulaid are lifted."

A DARK VISION

etanta settled down to sleep again but his eyes were barely closed when he woke up a third time in shock.

"Mother, I had another dream. This one was the worst:

"There were three ugly hags. They had cooked an animal. They offered me some but I didn't want to eat it. They were mocking me and laughing at me.

"Then there was a young girl washing a tunic at the river. She lifted it up. I counted twenty seven holes in it.

"Then the enemy army were there, all surrounding me. There were two black crows up above me. One of the crows came down and landed on my shoulder. What does it mean?"

Deichtire answered, "The first part is this: It is the custom of the Ulaid never to refuse a feast when it is offered. This dream is a warning to you never to break that bond. To save your honour: whenever the bread of friendship is offered, you must always stop to eat.

"The second part I don't know what it is. It is nothing at all, just a bad dream. Forget about it and go back to sleep."

But Deichtire did indeed know what the visions of the Washing of the Tunic and the flight of the Crows of War foretold for her son. Out of dread for the future, she lay awake all of the night. When morning came she sobbed wretchedly into her pillow until it was drenched through with her tears.

SETANTA RETURNS

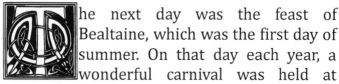he next day was the feast of Bealtaine, which was the first day of summer. On that day each year, a wonderful carnival was held at Emain Macha. There were fire-eaters. A mock battle was held at the ramparts. All day long the boy troop took part in a great blitz of hurling. That was the day that Setanta returned to the warrior school and there he made his oath for King Conchobar.

The lads were happy to see him and he was as happy to be back amongst them. They all lifted him up and carried him about the place, and afterwards threw him in the pond. They jumped in after him laughing. All except for the brother of the boy who was killed before. He stayed back, looking sullen. Finally he sulked off to sit on his bed alone, to play with his toy dagger.

Now there was a blacksmith called Culain

who had made ready a feast for King Conchobar, then went to Emain Macha to invite him.

He said, "Mighty King Conchobar! It would be my great privilege to hold a lavish feast in your honour, for you and your champions to attend. Will you accept my invitation?"

"I will."

"I am greatly honoured. May I ask one thing of you?"

"Go on."

"Respectfully, may I ask that you bring no more than fifty guests with you— only the truest and greatest of your men? The reason is this:

"All that I own, I have earned by my own sweat. I have the means to feed this number and no more in a grand manner, so that the night is fit to be called a king's feast."

"It is a good thing you ask Culain, my

friend. I will do this for you."

When the evening of Culain's feast came, the king put fine clothes on that were light for travelling. He took with him fifty chiefs and guards. Among them were heroes and champions: Dubhtach the Beetle was there; and Fergus of the Great Horse; and Conall the Victorious, who was the king's Champion of Champions; and Cathbad the Druid was there, who was the king's own father and the greatest druid in the land.

As the great train of horses and chariots was being prepared to leave Emain Macha, Conchobar went with Fergus down to the playing fields where the boy–troop were. The men laughed in amazement at what they saw there:

Three times fifty of the boys were at one end of the pitch and at the other end was Setanta, half their height, playing against them all. When they each took turns in goal, not one of them saved his shots from going in.

When he went into goal and they took turns shooting, he saved every shot. Even when all three fifties of them took a shot at the same time, he caught all the balls on his hurley, or on his chest, or on his arms or legs, so that not one shot got over the line.

When they played at wrestling, he would throw three times fifty boys to the ground under him and even all of them together could not lift him up off the ground.

"Look at the speed and strength of that little lad," laughed Conchobar.

"When he grows to his full height, his deeds will grow with him," said Fergus.

"Come here, wee hard man," called Conchobar. "Come with us to Culain's feast."

"I'm not finished my game."

"There is no time for that. Come on now lad!"

"You go on. I'll come after you when I'm

finished here."

Conchobar shook his head, laughing, "That's no way to talk to your king! We're away now. It is a fair way away and we'll be racing to get there. If you're wanting to catch up, you'd better be quick!"

THE FEAST OF CULAIN

onchobar and his train arrived at the house of Culain the Smith. There they were showered in gifts and honours. The finest of foods were served:

There were fresh chops of lamb, or the choicest cuts of loin of beef; there were smoked ribs of pork smothered in herbs and honey; there were cured apricots and pomegranates and sun-dried tomatoes that were brought in by boat from Spain.

From the same boat there were flagons of dark wine that tasted of berries. There was enough of that to keep all of their cups topped up to overflowing.

After the last of the food was served, the harpists struck up. Plates were cleared away. Tables were moved back to make room for dancing. Culain the Smith came up to Conchobar and asked, "King Conchobar, are all of your party here? Is there anyone else coming to follow you tonight?"

"No, we are all here. Why do you ask, my good friend?"

"I need to let out my guard dog to protect my cattle. A fine, loyal, fierce dog he is. It takes three chains to keep him down, with three men holding each chain. He has the strength of a hundred. His bite would take the leg off a horse. When I set him loose, no living thing will dare to come near the place, for he would tear them to pieces."

"I see. Set the dog loose then. Let the feast go on. What a grand feast it is too!"

But Conchobar had forgotten about the little lad who was still making his way there, in the last of the evening light.

To shorten his journey, the boy had made up a game: he would throw his ball up and throw his hurley after it, so that it hit the ball in the air. Then he would throw his staff up to hit the hurley and push it onwards so that the hurley hit the ball a second time, still in the air.

The guard dog was loosed to make his rounds of the dun fort. He came back round to the gate. He jumped up to his sitting–spot on a low hill nearby. There he lay down with his great jaw resting on his paws. He was as wild and furious and savage and ferocious and ready–for–a–fight a dog as there ever was. The beast peered out into the darkness. There he spied the little lad in the distance, coming closer.

The hound stood up. He let out a dreadful howl that echoed round the hills, sending shivers through the bones of all that heard it. He jumped off his watching–spot and hurtled towards the boy. His jaw hung slack. Slobbers flew everywhere. He looked like he might not bother ripping the child to pieces but just swallow him in one gulp instead.

Inside Culain's house, the talking stopped as the people listened to the mad din of howling and barking coming from outside. Conchobar jumped up in shock remembering, "The wee lad! He was to follow us!"

Conchobar's men all burst out from where they were, knocking over furniture; jumping over fences, to get to Setanta before he was killed.

CUCHULAIN GETS HIS NAME

ut on the road, Setanta watched the hound bearing down on him but, he didn't stop his game, or even skip a step. He threw his hurley and his staff up into the air, leaving himself without them for protection.

Then he picked up his little bronze ball, took aim at the hound, and threw it so hard that the ball went straight down the gullet of the beast and out his backside, pulling half his guts through with it.

The creature was mortally wounded for sure, but in his rage he hardly noticed. He charged on until he was right upon the boy.

But Setanta leapt up on to the beast's back. He hopped off again landing behind. He grabbed up the hound's back legs. Next the lad swung the beast round and round; faster, faster still; so that the beast's front paws flew up and his tongue flapped about.

With a mighty heave, Setanta lifted the hound up over his head and brought him down again. He dashed the beast on the stone ground so that his brain burst right out of his skull and all his bones smashed into bits all over the ground.

As Setanta stood over the body of the hound; Fergus, Conchobar and the other men rushed up. Fergus lifted the little lad from the ground on to the slope of his shoulder, then carried him to Conchobar. The king took his nephew on his knee. He hugged him. He kissed his head, overcome with joy that the boy had survived.

But Culain the Smith came out. When he saw his hound in pieces, his heart beat loudly against his breast. "I am glad, strong wee man, that you are safe, for your mother's sake.

"But it is bad luck for me that my dog is gone. He was a loyal, true friend. If it weren't for him, my herds and flocks and all of my goods would have been stolen long ago.

"Now that you have destroyed him, I have

no protection for my home.

The lad answered, "Don't worry about that. I will sort it out for you."

"And just how will you do that?" asked Culain.

"If you find me a pup of the same breed, I will rear it for you. I will train it to be fiercer than even this one was. Until he is big enough, I will guard your land myself. No-one will carry off a single calf or lamb or a bail of straw while I am here to stop them."

"That is a good offer," said Conchobar.

Cathbad the Druid declared, "Then let the child take the name:

"Cu Chulain – The Wolfhound of Culain!"

"I like my own name better: Setanta, son of Sualtaim," said the boy.

But Cathbad replied, "That may be, but still I forsee that the men of Erin will know the name Cuchulain for all of time. Great will be the deeds of the man in his full strength, who did this at just six years old."

"Then that is a good name too," said the boy.

In this way the name Cuchulain stuck to the lad. That is the name by which he is remembered to this day; and his later deeds were great indeed, as great as any that have been.

CUCHULAIN TAKES UP ARMS

hen Cuchulain was seven years old, he decided to spy on Cathbad the Druid, who was teaching the magical art of divination to his pupils. One of the pupils asked,

"Cathbad, tell us, what is today good for?"

So Cathbad set out his signs of power before him, in order to read their meaning.

But when he looked there, he frowned.

"I see the night sky: clear and dark. The stars have risen: There the Hunter, the Queen, the Bull. A flash of white— a shooting star! Lastly, now the faint stars of the Milky Way: countless, unnamed...

"Today is a day of dark fortune indeed! I pity the mother whose son takes up arms today. For he that does will become famous beyond imagining. The light of his fame will shine brighter than any other. His glory will live forever.

"But the light that shines brightly is one that burns fiercely. I forsee that the price of such fame is a life cut short. He will die even before he reaches his full strength!"

When Cuchulain heard this, he rushed to King Conchobar and said,

"Conchobar, fine and wonderful king. You are the greatest king the Ulaid have known!"

"That is a well prepared greeting," replied Conchobar, "I think someone is angling after a favour... What is it you want, young man?"

"I will take up arms today!"

The king laughed, "I don't think so! You're not ready for that for a good many years yet! What in the name of Brigit put that idea in your head?"

"Cathbad the Druid said it after looking at his druid signs."

"Did he indeed? I see. Well, Cathbad sees further than anyone. It is not wise to go against his advice. Come, let us choose your weapons."

So the king led Cuchulain to the armoury and handed him a spear.

Cuchulain bent the spear to test it but it exploded into splinters. He took another but the same thing happened. In the same way, the lad got through fifty spears. Before long, he was standing in the middle of a big pile of broken hardwood. At last, Conchobar gave him his own spear to try, which was called *Fíoreitilt – True of Flight*. Cuchulain could not bend it.

Next Cuchulain picked up a tall shield. He swung it around roughly to get a feel for it; but it burst open at the rivets and fell to bits. He took up another, then another; but the same thing happened to each. So Conchobar offered him his own shield. It was dark and wide; forged of bronze with gilded rims. Its name was *Níbhrisfidh – Unbreakable.* But it was heavy, so that few fully grown men were able to even lift it. Cuchulain squeezed it and swung it and span it. It took the strain.

In the same way, Cuchulain tested many of the best swords of Emain Macha; but they all ended up blunted or buckled or split or snapped.

Then Conchobar said, "Try this one."

He unsheathed his own sword and raised it high.

"This is *Fionog – Squall Crow!* He is the sword of swords. He puts horror on all enemies he meets; for once he is unsheathed in anger, he'll not stop until he catches his foe!"

Conchobar threw the sword to Cuchulain.

"These arms are good," said the little boy, "they suit me well."

"They are yours from this day, young warrior, though it hurts me to part with them. May they bring you long luck in battle and a swift end to your rivals!"

Then Cathbad arrived and said in shock, "Has the young hound taken up arms? It's a bad day for that!"

"He has!" replied Conchobar, "but he told me you put him up to it. I can see now that he lied to me!"

"It was no lie!" shouted Cuchulain. "It was Cathbad put it into my head. He said that the young man who takes up arms today will be famous for all time and his life will be short! That is the life for me. I'd rather be the hero who died, than a nobody who lived!

"I will not have a coward's death: in my bed with grey hair and a full belly. Give me instead the death of a hero: standing in the field of battle, my sword in my hand! Even if it means my life is to end this very day, I would not change it!"

Cathbad nodded. "So be it, Cuchulain. You have chosen your path. There can be no stepping off it now. Yet I hope, for the sake of Deichtire, that that road is longer than the signs predict."

"I need a chariot!" said Cuchulain.

"You do indeed," agreed Conchobar, "You can take mine: the strongest and fastest chariot in all the land. That way we can skip the wrecking of all the others! Where is my man, Ibar?"

So Ibar, the king's charioteer, was fetched and he took Cuchulain out.

"Take me to the playing fields, Ibar," said Cuchulain.

When they got there the boy troop stopped their games and all ran up to him. "Cuchulain has taken up arms!" they cheered, "Good luck to you Cuchulain! We'll miss you now that your time playing games is finished!"

Ibar and Cuchulain did the circuit of Emain three times, with the boy troop chasing behind and clouds of dust rising into the air.

Then Ibar said, "Young lad, it is time for the horses to be let out to pasture. Tomorrow I will take you out on your first adventure."

"No Ibar, take me out on the road now!"

"Where to?"

"As far as the highway takes us!"

"You are keen!" said Ibar. So he whipped the horses up to a gallop and didn't let them slow down until they reached Ath na Foraire – The Ford of Watching, at the foot of Sliabh Fuait.

Ath na Foraire was the place where a champion of the Ulaid would guard the high road to Emain Macha. Should a stranger, carrying arms, arrive on the road without good cause, the champion would challenge them to battle.

Or should a poet arrive at the ford in need of rest, or be leaving the kingdom carrying a grudge against the king, then the champion would feed him well, and load him up with treasure so that the poet would sing the praises of the Ulaid: their greatness and their honour, wherever he travelled.

On that night, Conall Cernach, The Victorious, was on duty at the ford. He waved the chariot down, "Well, Ibar! Has the young hound taken up arms today?"

"He has," said Ibar.

"I think he's too short for that! Sure he looks hardly able to tie up his own boots."

Cuchulain disagreed, "Go on home now Conall. I'll guard the Ford tonight."

"You will not, Cuchulain. Sure there's no way you're fit to stand up against fighting men. I'll stay put here. Good luck to you anyway!"

"Then I'll travel on to Lough Echtran," said Cuchulain, "I might redden my hand there."

"Then I'd better come along with you," said Conall, "If I let you come to harm, all of Uladh will be calling for my head."

"Come on, Ibar!" shouted Cuchulain, intent

to get away fast.

But Conall jumped in his chariot and came racing up behind them. So Cuchulain picked up a rock the size of his fist and threw it hard and low, so that it cracked the stock of Conall's chariot. The wheels span off. The chariot flipped over.

"What did you do that for?" roared Conall.

"You'll not be able to follow me now!" laughed Cuchulain.

"Bad luck to your throw! And bad luck to you! Whoever you meet tonight can take your head off for all I care!" said Conall, before he sulked back to the ford.

Ibar drove the horses south to Lough Echtran. But when they got there they found no-one.

"Let us go back home now, Cuchulain! It is getting late and I am hungry. It is all very well for you, the king's nephew. Your seat is kept for you at the king's table. As for me, I have to fight it out for my share among the messengers and the poets."

"Lazy Ibar! We are not done yet! Bring me to that mountain up ahead. Teach me the names of the places of Uladh and beyond."

So Ibar drove them to the heights of Sliabh Moduirn and to Finncairn – the White Cairn, which was the seeing–place at its peak.

From there they looked out over the vast rolling plains of Mag Brega. Far in the distance, the waters of the Bóinne river twinkled silver in the evening sun.

"See there, boy," pointed Ibar, "is the great Dun of Aengus at Brú na Bóinne. There is Ceannanas; there Teamhrach; there Cletech and Cnogba and there the Brug Fort of Mac In Oc."

"What is that dark place there north of Teamhrach?" asked Cuchulain.

"That is the dun fort of the Mac Necht Scene – the three sons of Necht. They are the most dangerous of all of the enemies of the Ulaid, since their father was killed in battle at the hand of King Conchobar."

"Let us go there now!" decided Cuchulain.

"We will not. It would be a deadly mistake to venture there, wee man. Not even Conall the Victorious, the Champion of Champions, would dare to go within a mile of that dun unless he had fifty fighting men at each side of him. Between them, the three sons of Necht have killed more men of the Ulaid than there are now left living. A swift death is waiting for whoever goes there, but it will not be me."

"Bad Ibar! I came out tonight to redden my sword with the blood of an enemy. Living or dead, you'll take me there now."

"Alive I will go with you, daring young fellow. But it is dead I will leave there." He yoked the horses and they pushed on towards the dun.

CUCHULAIN DRAWS HIS SWORD

They reached the dun of the three sons of Necht Scene. The boy sprang out of the chariot and ran up to the pillar-stone that had been placed on the green. There were Ogham marks carved into the stone.

"Read the marks to me, Ibar. What do they say?"

"They say this:

'Whatever champion comes to this place, he may not leave without first giving single combat.'"

Cuchulain put his two arms around the pillar-stone, pulled it out of the ground, and threw it with an enormous splash into the river.

Ibar shook his head, "It was better off where it was before. You will surely get now what you came here looking for: a fast end to your short life."

"Good Ibar. I am tired. Spread the blankets down for me so I can catch a bit of sleep."

"This is a bad place to stop, Cuchulain," Ibar said as he pulled the covers over the lad.

"Now don't wake me up if just one person comes out. If two or three come, I will deal with them," said Cuchulain. Then he turned over and went to sleep.

Ibar stayed alert. He held the reins of his horses in his hand so that he could get away quicker. He kept a good eye on the gate of the fort.

The gate opened and Foill, son of Necht walked out. "Are those the banners of Conchobar of Emain Macha I see tied to your chariot? And are those his speckled horses?" he shouted.

"They are," answered Ibar, terrified.

"Don't unyoke those horses here unless it's a fight you are after! Which champion of Emain with you there dares to stop at the fort of Mac Necht Scene— we who have killed more of your people than we allowed to live? Show yourself!"

"I haven't unyoked the horses. See, I am holding the reins still. It is just a child with me here. He took up arms today for good luck, and now he is sleeping."

"If he were a fully grown fighting man, he would be a dead one by now. But child or not, I might kill him anyway."

"It would be against your honour to do that. He is not fit to fight against the likes of you."

But Cuchulain heard what was said about him. He burst out of his bed, red with disdain, "I am fit to fight!"

"I think you are not, you puny little wretch! You look like you still need your mother to tuck you into bed," laughed the man.

Then Cuchulain challenged him, "Go and get your weapons, you big ham! It would be bad luck for me to kill an unarmed man."

Foill had heard enough. He ran back to the fort to arm himself for battle.

But Ibar warned, "Be careful, Cuchulain. That man is Foill, son of Necht, and neither spear nor sword can harm him!"

"Don't worry about that," shrugged Cuchulain, "I will use the shield trick on him."

So Cuchulain lifted his little bronze ball and fired it at the man. It bounced off the top of the man's shield, and hit him in the head. It carried on out the other side, taking with it a lump of the man's brain the size of an apple. It left behind a hole that the light of the sky shone through. Cuchulain sliced off the man's head as his prize.

Next, the second son of Necht ran out shouting, "I suppose you are boasting about that deed!"

"I see no cause to boast about killing just the one man," answered Cuchulain.

"Well you'll not be boasting about anything for much longer, brat, for I'll kill you in a minute."

Then Cuchulain challenged him, "Go and get your weapons, you useless cow pat! Sure only a coward comes out of his fort unarmed, you stinking pile of horse mess!"

But Ibar warned him again, "Cuchulain you are in mortal danger now! That man is Tuachall the Cunning, the second son of Necht. In battle he moves faster than the eye can follow. He guides the point of his sword with such precision that he will disarm you before you even know it has happened!

"If he is not killed outright with the first throw of the spear, he can't be killed at all."

"It is a good thing that you told me that, Ibar. I will put the spear of Conchobar through him before he gets a chance to use his skills of cunning on me—or on anyone else ever again."

Tuachall charged the lad. He wore his heavy armour. He held his shield high to fend off the spear throw.

Cuchulain launched the longspear *Fíoreitilt – True of Flight* high into the air and it came down hard on the shield of Tuachall. The force of the throw cleaved the shield into halves. The spear passed straight through the middle. It split the bronze chestplate of Tuachall's armour and its spear–tip stopped inside the chambers of the man's heart. Cuchulain took off the man's head before the heart had stopped beating and before his body had hit the ground.

The third son of Necht Scene came out and challenged Cuchulain, "Upstart! Follow me unarmed into the deepest part of the river. I will fight you hand to hand. For killing my brother Foill, you will pay with your life! Then I will take the life of your charioteer to pay for the death of Tuachall."

The lad mocked him, "Get away, you big bunch of flowers. I'll rip your skinny girl's arms off and slap you round your big baby head with them. Your mammy changes your nappy!"

Ibar warned once again, "Cuchulain, please don't go into the water, this is a trick. Jump into the chariot now. There is time yet for us both to get away alive.

"That man is Fandall, son of Necht, who is called *The Swallow*. He moves over the water faster than the swallow flits. There is not a swimmer in the world can keep up with him, yet he has the strength of a crocodile. When he catches you, he will pull you under. He will drag you down until you are trapped up in the underwater weeds. That will surely be the end of you and the end of me."

"That doesn't worry me too much, Ibar. Don't you know that at the end of a day of sport at Emain, when the lads jump into the river to cool down, then this is the feat I like to perform: I take one boy on each of my shoulders, and one on each of my palms. Then I carry them all from the deepest part of the water to the edge, without hardly getting my knees wet!"

Cuchulain laid down his arms. He ran to the river, made a mighty salmon leap and dived under. Fandall treaded far out in the water waiting for him to surface.

After ten minutes the lad still hadn't come up for air. Fandall waited. Ibar feared the worst.

After half an hour had passed, there was still no sign of the lad, not even a single breath bubble. Fandall laughed, "He wasn't much of a swimmer. The water took him before I could get near him. Come you into the water now, charioteer, I will—"

Just at that moment, Cuchulain burst out of the water behind Fandall and dragged him underneath. There he dug his heels into the man's neck, while he squeezed the man's head between his bare hands. He popped the man's head off his body like it was a cork coming off a bottle. The body floated off down the river.

Cuchulain and Ibar raided the fort of Mac Necht Scene. When they were done, they set it on fire. They stood watching as it burned to the ground, sending up clouds of black smoke that could be seen as far away as Emain Macha.

Finally, they left the dun fort of Mac Necht Scene, carrying its treasure inside the chariot, and the heads of the three great warriors tied to the front.

When Ibar reached Sliabh Fuait, a herd of wild deer crossed their path.

"What are those strange cattle, Ibar?" asked Cuchulain.

"Child, they are not cattle! They are wild deer that run freely in the woods of Oircil, between Sliabh Fuait and Sliabh Gullion. The meat of these deer is as tender as any in Erin."

"What is the best way to catch them, alive or dead?"

"Few can catch them at all, and no one has ever caught one alive."

"Catch up with them then, Ibar. I will bring down one or two of them. We will take them home alive."

Ibar spurred on the horses to gallop as fast as they could run, but even then the deer were too fast and too nimble, and the chariot could get nowhere near them.

So Cuchulain leapt out and ran on faster than the horses. He ran up beside the biggest of the stags, grabbed it by the antlers, then pulled it down to the ground. He pressed its head into the ground with one hand. Then using his free hand only, he grabbed a second stag as it bounded by. He bundled up both the animals into his arms.

They kicked and bellowed and slashed and lashed out at him. But he carried them back to the chariot and tied them down.

They carried on their journey back to Emain Macha. A little further on, a flock of white birds flew overhead.

"What are those birds, Ibar?" asked Cuchulain.

"They are wild swans. They come in from the rocks and crags of the great sea to feed on the plains and sheltered places of Emain."

"Would it be better to catch them alive or dead?" Cuchulain wondered.

"Neither way, lad," said Ibar, "they cannot be caught alive or dead these swans. They fly too high to hit in the air. When they land, they are wary of people, so no-one can get close enough for a shot."

"I will catch them alive then," decided Cuchulain.

He put eight small stones into his sling and performed a feat: he cast the stones high, hit eight of the birds which fell to the ground, stunned but alive.

Then he performed a greater feat: he put another eight small stones into his sling; so brought down a further *sixteen* birds with a single cast.

"Jump out of the chariot, Ibar, and collect the birds. If I leave you here alone with the wild stags, they'll have you stuck on their antlers dead before I get back."

"No, I couldn't do that lad. We are moving too fast! If I jump out the side, I'll get cut to pieces by the wheels; or if I jump out the front, I'll get trampled by the horses; or if I go out the back, I'll get gored on the antlers of the stags and killed!"

"You are no good of a warrior, Ibar! This is what I will do: I will fix the stags with such a stare that they will bend their heads in fear and awe of me. Then you can go out over the antlers safely."

So Cuchulain eyeballed the stags. They

bowed their heads in terror. Ibar climbed out of the chariot, stepping over the antlers of the cowed animals. He recovered the swans, which were starting to wake up. He tied them to the back of the chariot on long leashes.

They raced through Ath na Foraire – The Ford of Watching, without slowing down. Cuchulain shook his spear and roared at Conall the Victorious,

"It's a full moon!"

Then he bared the cheeks of his backside out the side of the chariot; a grossly insulting gesture. Conall was forced to dive into the water to avoid being run over. In this way the boy and the man charged on triumphantly, boastingly, battle–reddened to Emain Macha, with the wild swans tumbling above them as a blur of white.

As they came into view of the great fort at Emain Macha, the king's messenger Lebharcham watched their approach from the

spy tower. She raced in terror to Conchobar shouting, "Close the gates! We are under attack!

"A champion is heading this way with a terrible fury on him. The warrior's light is around him!

"He has the heads of his enemies swinging in front of him. Above him and around him are many wild birds flying, yet bound to the chariot. Behind him are wild, untamed stags, leaping and roaring."

Conchobar said, "That must be the boy returning. His blade must be wetted. If his fighting frenzy can't be brought down, there will be slaughter at Emain this night!"

So they came up with a plan to meet Cuchulain and calm his rage.

Cuchulain arrived at the gates. He turned the left side of his chariot towards the gate in defiance, and rattled his spear against his shield.

He was berserk with anger, and no longer able to separate friend from foe.

He screeched out a challenge: "Send out a champion to meet me in battle! Send him out now, or I swear I will come in to spill the blood of every man in the fort!"

He raced the chariot around the gate, carving circles in the dust. His eyes rolled white in his head. He growled and roared and screamed and howled like a pack of wild wolves, starving and demented.

Then the gates of the fort opened, but the champions of Emain did not come forth. Instead, out streamed three times fifty of the women of Emain Macha: young and old. They smiled and laughed and sang; they waved their arms in welcome.

They came dancing and skipping towards Cuchulain where he stood. They surrounded him. They closed around him. They put their arms over him all at once. They patted his shoulders and chest. They stroked his hair down and smothered his cheeks in kisses.

Cuchulain stood stunned, quivering. He gripped his spear and shield on account of his boiling rage, but was unable to move a muscle for fear of hurting any one of the women.

Together the mothers and daughters of Emain raised Cuchulain above their heads. They shared his weight among them so that their many hands were like a stretcher beneath him. There he lay, as they bore him through the gates, towards the first of the vats of cold water they had prepared. They plunged him under.

But the water whistled and turned to steam. The vat burst its staves and its hoops like the cracking of nuts around him.

They dunked him in the second vat. It boiled up with bubbles as big as fists until it was dry.

They lifted him once more and lowered him into the third vat. This time, the water heated up enough to cook with, but it didn't overflow. Cuchulain wiped the drips of water from his brow. He grinned, "Have you a bite to eat? I'm starving."

His wrath was gone. In its place, his *Glow of Victory* came over him. His skin shone purple and magenta. His golden halo surrounded him. His face became so beautiful that the women around him gasped and their hearts swooned.

Seven pupils shone from each of his two princely eyes. Four brilliant gems: of emerald and sapphire; of ruby and diamond, was each separate pupil.

He stood up and the women draped a fine green cloak around him. They placed a silver pin at his shoulder to hold the cloak closed. The pin shone too brightly to look at. A hood of purple velvet, threaded with gold, was put around his neck. A crown of silver was placed on his head. It gleamed like the morning sun. The little lad sat down at the feet of Conchobar, who was on his high throne, and that was his sitting–place thereafter.

King Conchobar declared, "The Hound of the Ulaid is truly a wonder! His triumph today is as promising a debut as ever has been! Have no doubt, those of his future will be many and glorious and even greater still!" Everyone agreed.

And so ends the true story of the boyhood deeds of Cuchulain. Remember that he displayed these astonishing feats at the mere age of seven. Just imagine what he went on to achieve at the age of seventeen...

ABOUT THE TUATH DE DANANN

The strange people of the Tuath Dé Danann, who are ever young, are the magical race who live in that invisible otherworld that is right beside you, close enough to touch, but at the same time far away, so that no-one who finds their way there can ever return.

In Cuchulain's day, the Tuath Dé Danann were known as the Sidhe. This was also the name they gave to their houses. The houses were wide mounds with tall stone doors and low earthen roofs that would appear in the middle of the countryside out of nowhere. Then, just when everyone was getting used to them being there, they would vanish without a trace.

In those days the people of the Sidhe would move freely between their world and Cuchulain's, watching the lives of the men of Erin. Some of the Sidhe were generous: they shared their gifts of music and of wisdom with the mortal people. But others of them were bad–tempered: any man or woman unlucky enough to cross them could find themselves turned into a pig or a weasel or a fly. They loved to create mischief among the people, for fun, and they all (except for one) loved the people of Erin as much as a mother loves her children.

The full story of how the Tuath Dé Danann came to the island of Erin is told elsewhere, in *The Book of the Taking of Ireland*, and also in the *Annals of the Four Masters*. Here is a much shortened version:

They arrived all at once, on six times fifty sailing ships, led by King Nuada of the Silver Arm. When they landed they fell instantly in love with their new land, with its lush forests and with its many glittering lakes. King Nuada declared that the island of Erin would be the place that the Tuath Dé would call home from that time on. So as never to forget their vow, they burned all of their ships.

But the Tuath Dé Danann did not have the country to themselves. Settled across the land before them were the Firbolg, a great warrior race whose seat of power was at Teamhrach (which is now called Tara) in the East.

A battle was fought between the Tuath Dé Danann and the Firbolg. But the Tuath Dé Danann's power was greater. They had the Morrigna, who cast spells of battle to blind the Firbolg. In the confusion that followed, the Tuath Dé pushed deep and won the fight. After the battle was over, the kings of the two sides talked and an agreement was made: their peoples would share the island. The Tuath Dé took the greater part, including the Fort of Kings at Teamhrach, while the Firbolg took the kingdom of Connacht in the West.

Even then, the Tuath Dé were not free to claim lordship of the land, because the Firbolg had been terrorised by the Fomorians: a fierce, cruel race of giants and half-giants, who inhabited the small islands that were scattered along the coast of Erin. The greatest of the Fomor was Balor of the Evil Eye. He could kill a hundred men using just the power of his gaze. In the past, the giants had forced the Firbolg to pay a third of their grain and milk in tribute. But worse than this, they would take away every third Firbolg child to be a slave. This same dreadful tax the Fomor now demanded of the Tuath Dé Danann.

King Nuada refused to accept this. And so, a terrible war was fought between the Tuath Dé Danann and the ruling Fomorians.

The mightiest battle that the country would ever see took place at Mag Tuired, in the West. In that battle, every living man from every corner of the island took part. It raged on for seventy days, with awful slaughter brought upon both sides, but neither army was able to gain the upper hand. So dreadful was the fighting at Cath Mag Tuired that it became known as the Last Battle—in order that no-one would forget the harm that was done, and the heavy price that was paid for the win.

At the end of Cath Mag Tuired, Balor of the Evil Eye fought King Nuada and killed him. Without their king to lead them, Nuada's army suddenly lost heart, and the war was all but lost.

But Lugh of the Long Hand, who was King Nuada's Champion, battled on until he came between his fallen king and the enemy Balor. The army of the Tuath Dé rallied once again around Lugh and began to push the Fomorians back. Then Balor unveiled his evil eye.

Standing on top of the Hill of Rath, looking over the plain of battle, Balor shouted to his guards to haul on the ropes that lifted the heavy eyelid. A deadly slit appeared. On the hillside below him, the men of the Tuath Dé Danann began dropping dead where they stood. But before its full power could be revealed, Lugh fired a stone from his slingshot into the half–opened eye. The force of the stone put the eye out through the back of the head. The eyeball rolled over and over, down the back of the hill. Its deadly beam swept over the ranks of the Fomor. Lines of giants fell dead like runs of dominos.

The Fomorians that escaped the evil glare all scattered and ran. The giants didn't stop running until they reached their ships. They sailed back to their islands and stayed there. The Tuath Dé Danann had at last won the kingship of Erin, and paid tax to no-one after that.

But the story of the Tuath Dé Danann does not end there. *The Book of the Taking of Ireland* also tells of the coming of the Gaels (who were also called the Milesians.) The Gaels were the ancestors of King Conchobar, and indeed of all of the people who lived in Cuchulain's day. They had settled across the five great kingdoms of Erin: Uladh, Mumha, Midhe, Laighin and Connacht.

The Gaels displaced the Tuath Dé not through war but through politics. Many of the Tuath Dé had been killed during the Last Battle against the Fomor. Perhaps, for those that lived in the aftermath of the war, their appetite for violence was diminished, having had time to weigh the freedom they had won against the lives it had cost them.

Furthermore, in the intervening ages, the magical powers of the Tuath Dé had grown immensely. At the same time, their thoughts had grown away from the quarrels of men, and into the deep, unknowable matters of gods. By the time the Gaels arrived, trifles such as kingship and wealth were no longer of concern to the now ever–young.

When the army of the Gaels arrived at the shores of Erin, a challenge was made to the Tuath Dé Danann:

"Hand over this land—every path, pillar and lintel—or we will take it from you by force."

The Tuath Dé Danann countered with a challenge of their own:

"Reboard your ships. Sail out to the distance of nine waves. Then turn your ships around and try to land once again. If you succeed, we will hand over our land to you freely, just as you demand: every step, every post, every arch."

The Gaels accepted the challenge. They hauled the anchors of their ships and sailed out of the bay until they were nine waves distant from the shore.

But Manannán of the Tuath Dé Danann, whose power lay with the tempest, sent a furious storm upon the Gaels to drive them away. The ships were rocked and buffeted. Their sails were torn to shreds. Their ropes and rigging were tangled. Water flooded the decks. Men were thrown overboard and drowned. The ships were blown this way and that, so that the armada was scattered apart and washed away from the land. The winds battered them relentlessly, so that they were pushed further out into the wide ocean, surely to be lost forever.

But the Gaels knew that the storm was the work of magic. So their druids prayed with magic of their own, to parry the attack; to cancel its power. Amergin, their leader, climbed to the prow of his ship. He fell to his knees, cast his arms out wide and chanted,

Sweet Ériu, fair of face,
Mother of this land
Of blessed bounty, nurtured by
Your ever–gentle hand.

Sweet Ériu, full of grace,
Spare us from our trial.
Deliver us from this evil torrent.
Shelter us awhile.

Sweet Ériu, fair in fortune,
Your welcome we would know.
Hear our prayer, we ask but this:
Strong roof, warm hearth,
A candle lit, a place to sit.
Praise you.

Amergin's words carried above the storm to Ériu – Queen of the Tuath Dé Danann. The words touched her heart, and told her that the time of passing had arrived. She placed her hand on Manannán's arm and looked into his eyes. This calmed his rage. The challenge was ended.

With this the storm blew itself out. The

waves rolled back, leaving the surface calm and flat. A light wind blew up behind the Gaels' ships, pushing them gently towards the land, their banners fluttering. Soon their keels bumped against sand.

Amergin jumped down. He led his army to the gates of Teamhrach, where they demanded their prize. But the Kings of the Tuath Dé Danann failed to keep their promise to hand over their country without a fight. They had no wish to be parted from their beloved Erin, and indeed could no longer leave her, even if they had wanted to— because all of their godly power was bound to her: threaded like quartz–veins through the bedrock of her mountains.

A final battle was fought at the plain of Tailtinn. The Tuath Dé fought as bravely as they ever had done. But the Gaels proved braver. The three kings of the Tuath Dé Danann were killed on the battlefield. They passed into the Otherworld. Their wives—Ériu, Banba and Fódla—passed through with them.

Then the three queens merged together

with the spirit of the land and with each other: three goddesses but at the same time one being—*a holy trinity*. The triple-goddess called to her people, and all of the Tuath Dé Danann passed over to her. From that time, none of them were—except on the rarest of occasions —seen abroad again.

After the vanishing of the Tuath Dé Danann, the Great Hall at the Fort of Kings belonged to the Gaels evermore, and the rest of the country with it.